Dig In!

words by
Cindy Jenson-Elliott

dirt by
Mary Peterson

TURNIP

Beach Lane Books
New York • London • Toronto • Sydney • New Delhi

For Ania,
who loves mud—C. J.-E.

To Josie,
in her garden, with pansies—M. P.

BEACH LANE BOOKS • An imprint of Simon & Schuster Children's Publishing Division • 1230 Avenue of the Americas, New York, New York 10020 • Text copyright © 2016 by Cindy Jenson-Elliott • Illustrations copyright © 2016 by Mary Peterson • All rights reserved, including the right of reproduction in whole or in part in any form. • Beach Lane Books is a trademark of Simon & Schuster, Inc. • For information about special discounts for bulk purchases, please contact Simon & Schuster Special Sales at 1-866-506-1949 or business@simonandschuster.com. • The Simon & Schuster Speakers Bureau can bring authors to your live event. For more information or to book an event, contact the Simon & Schuster Speakers Bureau at 1-866-248-3049 or visit our website at www.simonspeakers.com. • Book design by Lauren Rille • The text for this book is set in Apple Boy. • The illustrations were created using linoleum block prints on paper with some digital touch ups. • Manufactured in China • 1215 SCP • First Edition • 10 9 8 7 6 5 4 3 2 1 • Library of Congress Cataloging-in-Publication Data • Jenson-Elliott, Cynthia L., author. • Dig in! / Cindy Jenson-Elliott; illustrated by Mary Peterson.—First edition. • p. cm. • Summary: A little boy digs, plays, and explores in his garden. • ISBN 978-1-4424-1261-3 (hardcover) • ISBN 978-1-4424-4127-9 (eBook) • 1. Play—Juvenile fiction. 2. Gardens—Juvenile fiction. [1. Play—Fiction. 2. Gardens—Fiction.] I. Peterson, Mary (Mary Jeanette), illustrator. II. Title. • PZ7.J454Di 2016 • [E]—dc23 • 2014044124

I dig in the dirt . . .

and find a worm.

Worm wiggles.

I dig in the dirt . . .

and find a rock.

I dig in the dirt . . .

and find a pill bug.

Pill bug curls.

I dig in the dirt . . .

and find a seed.

Seed waits.

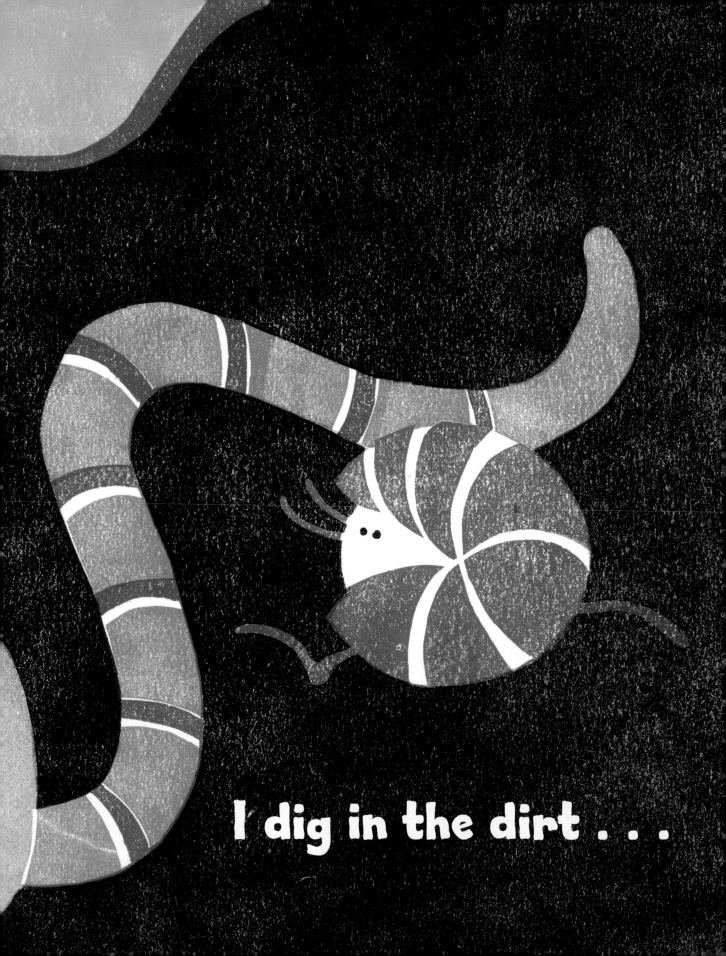

I dig in the dirt . . .

and find a spider.

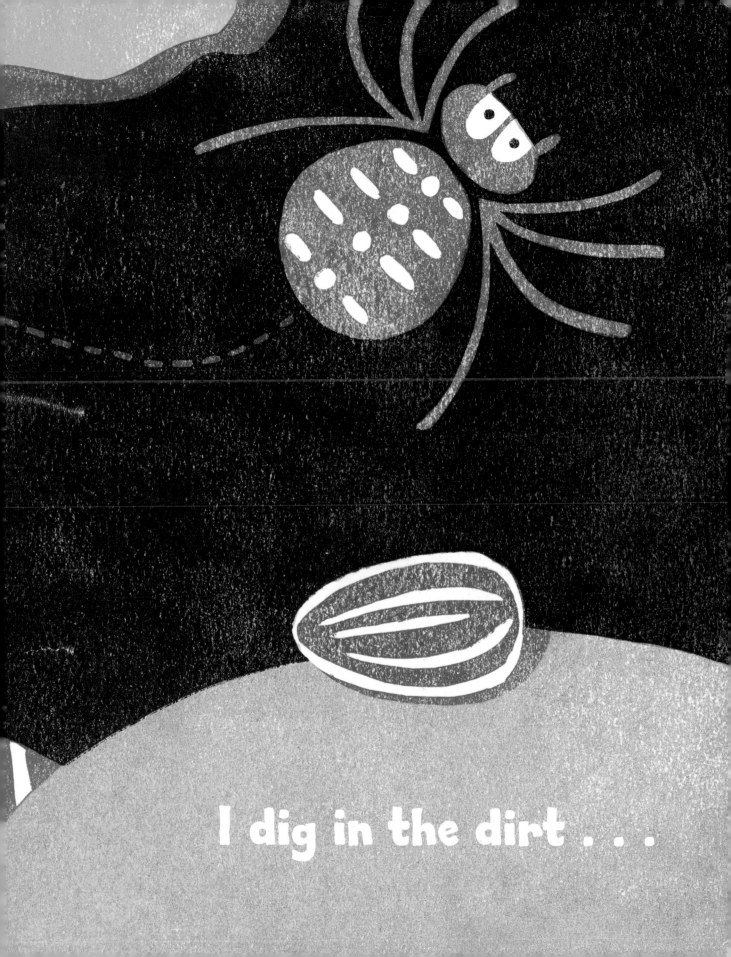

I dig in the dirt . . .

and find a sprout.

Sprout grows.

I dig in the dirt . . .

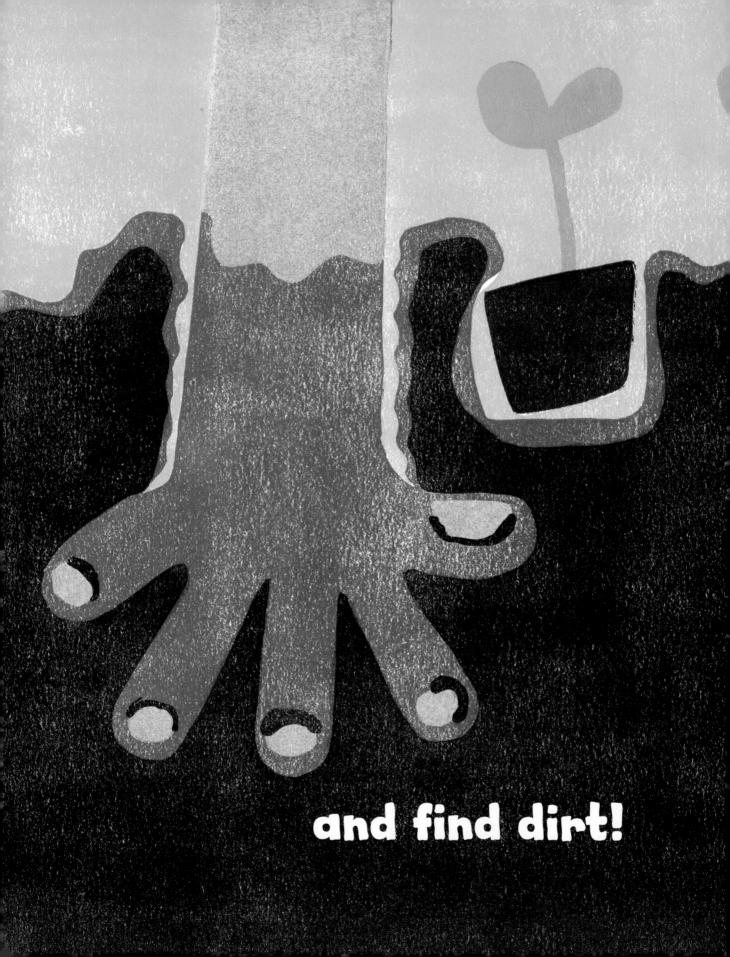

and find dirt!

Dirt squishes.

Then I water the dirt
and find . . .